Usborne
Illustrated Stories
from
China

Usborne
Illustrated Stories
from
China

Retold by
Rosie Dickins & Andrew Prentice

Illustrated by
Li Weiding

Contents

About the Stories

China is a huge country, with a very long history and a rich variety of story-telling traditions. This book contains a selection of stories from all over China, chosen especially to appeal to readers today.

About the Stories

The stories were originally created for many different reasons. Some were told simply to entertain, but others – such as "The Fox and the Tiger" and "The Frog in the Well" – were meant to teach people something about life. Sometimes, these stories captured an idea so perfectly that a phrase from them has become an everyday Chinese saying.

Some stories grew out of traditional festivals. For example, "The Mouse Wedding" and "The New Year Monster" are both linked to the Chinese New Year (also known as the Spring Festival). In China, this is the biggest celebration of the year, falling sometime around February – the exact date varies, as it depends on the cycles of the moon.

About the Stories

Only a few of the stories can be traced back to an original author. Most folk tales have been told and retold so often, in so many versions, that no one can be sure exactly how they began. Some old Chinese tales even share elements with old fairy tales told in Europe, showing how wide the influence of popular stories can be – just compare "The Golden Slippers" and "Cinderella," or "Great-Aunt Tiger" and "Little Red Riding Hood."

These stories continue the tradition of retellings, bringing the stories to a new audience in China and around the world.

About the
Illustrations

The illustrations in this book were painted in the traditional Chinese way, using a traditional-style brush and inks – the same materials you can see in the picture of an artist opposite. Chinese artists have been making paintings in this way for over two thousand years.

About the Illustrations

Chinese paintings are made quickly, with flowing hand movements, using a round brush dipped in watery ink. The finest, most delicate details are drawn in last, using only the very tip of the brush. Before paper was invented, artists painted on silk; nowadays, either paper or silk is used.

It takes great skill and years of study to perfect this way of painting. Chinese artists spend hours perfecting the precise brush movements needed to create each different shape and effect. Every movement has its own particular use – for example, when painting bamboo, a sideways dab with the bristles creates a neat leaf shape, while a quick flick makes a tapering stem.

12

About the Illustrations

The illustrator of this book, Li Weiding, was a famous artist and a professor of art in Shanghai, China. As deputy director of the Wen Hui Art Institute and honorary director of the Fenghua Calligraphy and Painting Institute, he became known throughout China for his skill and dedication to traditional Chinese painting.

In memory of Li Weiding,
1958-2018

This folk tale was first recorded in an ancient book titled "Strategies of Warring States," written to advise Chinese emperors and leaders.

The Fox and the Tiger

A long time ago, a fearsome tiger lived on a misty mountain. He prowled far and wide, high and low, gobbling up everything he saw. He was certain that no creature could challenge him for strength or good looks. He was particularly proud of his long tail and fine whiskers.

All the other creatures on the mountain lived in terror of the tiger's soft-footed approach and sharp, white teeth. They called him Silent Death, Lord of the Mountain.

The tiger thought this was right and proper. He marked the borders of his kingdom by scratching the trees and rocks with his claws. At night he roared at the moon, daring it to come down from the sky and fight him. But it never did.

One particularly fine morning, the tiger was stretched out on a rock, warming his back in the sun, when he heard a twig crack. Looking up, he was delighted to spot a red fox trotting, as bold as you like, between the yellow larch trees.

"Breakfast!" thought the tiger as he sprang into action. He raced between the trees, belly low, swift and silent. At the perfect moment, he pounced, pinning the little fox to the ground.

The tiger opened his mouth
to take a big bite.

"You are making a terrible
mistake," said the fox. "I wanted
to warn you."

The tiger was puzzled. He was used to animals
begging for their lives, or tearfully telling him to
take pity on their children. This fox just sounded,
well, bored.

"I beg your pardon," growled the tiger. "I see no
mistake here."

"Do you know who I am?" said the fox, raising
an eyebrow.

"You are a slow, stupid fox, soon to be eaten."

"Oh no," the fox chuckled. "I am the queen of
this mountain."

"What!" The tiger was so outraged that he let
the fox go. "That's ridiculous! Everyone knows

that I am the Lord of the Mountain. They call me Silent Death."

"That's very nice," smirked the fox as she dusted herself off. "Well done. But the Lord of Heaven himself has sent me to this mountain to be the new queen. If you gobble me up, he'll be very upset. It won't go well for you."

The tiger frowned. Of course he'd heard of the Lord of Heaven, the chief of the gods, but it was hard to imagine a god taking a close interest in who ruled this particular mountain, tall and majestic though it was.

"You can't prove this outrageous claim!" snarled the tiger. "I should just gobble you up."

"No need for that," said the fox. "Come with me, Silent Death, and I'll show you."

Still very puzzled, the tiger agreed. The pair of them walked off through the trees. The fox didn't bother to tread carefully, so all the animals had plenty of warning that they were coming. A herd of deer fled quickly, white tails bobbing. The birds screamed warnings from the trees. The crickets chirped and the marmots squeaked. Every animal that spied them got out of their way as quickly as possible.

All the time, the bold fox strutted in front of the tiger, puffing out her chest – and the tiger began to worry.

"Maybe there is something in her claim after all," he thought. "See how the other animals scamper away from her."

Suddenly the fox stopped dead. A beetle was crawling about in the leaves.

The fox bent down till her nose was right behind the unsuspecting beetle.

"Boo!" she said.

The beetle caught sight of both of them, rolled onto its back and pretended to be dead. This was too much for the tiger.

"Forgive me, Queen of the Mountain!" he shouted as he sprinted away, dodging off in strange directions so that the fox queen would find it hard to follow and get her revenge.

The fox chuckled quietly to herself as she gently turned the beetle the right way up.

"O Beetle! What a silly tiger," she said. "He didn't spot that the animals were terrified of him, not me. I suppose being bigger than everyone else doesn't mean you have a big brain too."

"All hail the Queen of the Mountain!" cheered the beetle. "Well done!"

The fox walked off into the woods, still laughing. The tiger never bothered her again.

This traditional tale tells the story of the Dragon King's daughter. In Chinese mythology, Dragon Kings are enormously powerful weather and water gods, who appear sometimes as dragons, sometimes as people.

The Pearl that Shone in the Dark

Mai Li, the eldest daughter of the Dragon King of the Eastern Sea, had a problem. She wanted to go on adventures and see the world. But all her father wanted her to do was sit in the palace and choose herself a husband.

On her father's orders, Chancellor Crab, Marshal Eel and General Flounder had scoured the country from north to south and east to west, hunting for suitable husbands. But all their scuttling and slithering and swimming did no good. The picky princess found fault with every noble suitor that they suggested.

"I don't want to marry someone who is rich and powerful," she insisted. "I want a man who is honest and brave."

Eventually, the Dragon King became exasperated with his daughter's quibbling. "You must choose a husband," he roared. "Or I will choose one for you!"

Mai Li decided to run away, rather than be forced into a marriage that she didn't want. Like all dragons she could change her shape at will, so she disguised herself as an old lady and left the

palace in secret. For months she journeyed far
and wide, hobbling along the roads with her
stick. She had many adventures, and met people
of all kinds.

One day, in wild country far to the west, she
came across Ah Shun, a poor farmer. Ah Shun
lived with his older brother, Ah Peng, in a
tumbledown hut. He didn't have much of
anything, but he was happy to share the little
that he had with a hungry old lady.

The princess watched Ah Shun in secret as
she ate the food he brought out. She couldn't help
noticing how he kept up a stream of funny jokes
to cover the fact that there wasn't enough rice for
both of them. She saw his kind manner, and the
warmth of his smile.

"Here is the man for me," Mai Li said to
herself. "I will marry no one else."

Determined, Mai Li returned to her father and told him of her decision. The king instantly changed into his dragon form. He tended to do that when angry.

"Faugh!" he roared, his eyes blazing. "You leave for months and now this foolishness! How can you be so sure this peasant is brave and honest? This is all most irregular."

"Ahem." Now Chancellor Crab sidled forward. "I have a plan, your majesty – if I might be so bold..."

When the chancellor had explained his idea, the Dragon King's horns glowed green and gold with delight. Even when they are upset, no dragon can resist a good ruse.

"Hah! A worthy test! And there's no way this peasant will pass it!" the king chuckled. "Truly you are called the most cunning of crustaceans."

"But if Ah Shun does pass it," said Mai Li, "I will marry him."

"Very well," agreed her father. "But he won't."

The following night, Ah Shun had a strange dream. An ancient, white-bearded crab scuttled into his hut.

"Wake up and go outside," said the crab urgently. "And your life will change."

Ah Shun woke with a cry, which roused Ah Peng who was sleeping beside him. When Ah Shun ran outside, his brother followed. The two men found a woman sitting beside the river bank. Her long hair trailed in the water, which gleamed like molten silver in the light of the full moon.

"Here's a pretty pickle!" The woman laughed to herself. "I wasn't expecting two of you!"

The brothers couldn't know it, but this was
Mai Li, the Dragon Princess herself.

As the princess looked the two brothers over,
Ah Shun admired the laughter in her eyes.

Ah Peng, however, had eyes only for her expensive clothes and jewels.

"So," said the princess, "as I've got both of you here, please tell me: which of you is the most honest and brave?"

"I am," replied both brothers with one voice.

"Then you will have to prove it," she said. "I will marry the man who can bring me a luminous pearl from the treasure house of the Dragon King of the Eastern Sea."

"But that's impossible," exclaimed the brothers. "The Dragon King lives at the bottom of the sea."

"Take these," said the woman – and she handed each brother a gold pin from her hair. "When the time comes, they will slice a path through the waves."

The two brothers set off at once.

Ah Peng grabbed their only
horse and went by the
Emperor's new road across the
mountains. Ah Shun pulled on
his battered straw sandals and took
the old, dusty track along the river.

In this way they journeyed far to the east, but
Ah Peng was always quicker.

As Ah Peng neared the coast, he came across a
village that was underwater. All the fields and
houses were flooded. It was still raining and the
villagers had taken refuge on high ground.

"Alas," they lamented. "If only we could
borrow the golden ladle from the Dragon King.
It has special powers over water – that's the only
way to get rid of this cursed flood."

Ah Peng overheard the villagers talking.

"I happen to be going that way myself," he

said airily. "I can fetch the golden ladle for you if you like. Now, I am very hungry – do you have any food?"

The villagers were overjoyed. Gratefully, they gave Ah Peng the last of their rice, and rowed him down the overflowing river to the sea.

Three days later, Ah Shun arrived in the village. It was still raining, and the waters had risen even higher. Ah Shun spent the rest of the day helping the villagers rescue their possessions from their flooded houses. While he helped them, he overheard much eager talk about the Dragon King's golden ladle.

"Funnily enough, I am going that way myself," he said. "Perhaps I could fetch it for you?"

After so much bad luck, the villagers were bewildered at this double good fortune. Here was another hero going to visit the Dragon King.

They didn't have any more food to give Ah Shun, but they gratefully accepted his offer, and begged the younger brother not to forget their plight.

"I won't forget you," promised Ah Shun. "And I will bring you this ladle as quickly as I can."

He refused to allow the villagers to row him down the river. Instead, he dived into the floodwaters and swam quickly and powerfully towards the ocean.

Soon he found his brother trembling beside the beach, watching the murderous waves. Giant walls of water crashed on the shore, biting boulders from the cliffs. Howling winds blew foam and spray through the air. The brothers could not know it, but General Flounder had been ordered by the Dragon King to make the ocean roar. For three long days Ah Peng had waited, far too scared to brave the violent water.

"The time has come," thought Ah Shun and pulled the golden hairpin from his pocket. Without a moment's hesitation, he threw himself into the water. To his astonishment, he didn't even get wet. The raging waves parted before him as if they had been sliced with a sword. Ah Shun landed on his belly on the wet sand. A few startled fish flopped nearby. He looked up and saw a wide path had opened up across the ocean floor.

"I-I was just waiting for you," said Ah Peng, who had nervously followed his brother across the sand.

Walking between the steepling walls of water, the two brothers soon arrived at the palace of the Dragon King. A squad of shrimp and crab soldiers were guarding the entrance.

The Pearl that Shone in the Dark

With their long whiskers trailing, a pair of shrimps escorted the brothers through a hundred ever-richer rooms, until they reached the jade throne of the king himself.

The coral-encrusted grandeur of the court was incredible to behold. Richly-robed salmon and starfish gaped at them as they walked past. A line of glowering lobsters guarded the throne. Their fearsome claws glinted in the soft light from a thousand delicately glowing anemones.

To the brothers' surprise, the Dragon King greeted them warmly and listened attentively as they explained why they had come so far. He seemed quite happy to let them have the run of his treasure house and only set one condition:

"My bold lads, you can choose any of my treasures that you like – but you may take one thing and one thing only. Choose well and wisely."

When the doors of the treasure house opened,
the brothers could hardly believe their eyes.
Riches from every country of the world and every
corner of the sea were gathered in great piles and
tumbled across tables and rugs: carved jade and
priceless porcelain, rare jewels and magic
weapons. Right in the middle of all the riches sat
a single, giant, glowing pearl.

Ah Peng rushed straight for the pearl. All he wanted was to marry the woman on the river bank. He snatched it up greedily. Glancing around, he longed to grab some other treasures too, but remembering the Dragon King's fierce warning, he touched nothing else and hurried back the way he had come.

Ah Shun had also spotted the luminous pearl but, remembering his promise to the flooded villagers, he asked to be given the golden ladle instead. Unfortunately, the ladle was small and rather hard to see amongst so much loot and no one was sure where it was. With such vast drifts of treasure to sift through, it took Ah Shun many hours to hunt the ladle down. At last he found it between the paws of a mechanical monkey.

After politely thanking the Dragon King for his generosity, Ah Shun walked back to the shore.

There he discovered that his brother was long gone. In fact, Ah Peng had already reached the flooded village. While they had been away, the waters had risen still further. All the crops had died and the buildings had been swept away.

A crowd of villagers rushed to Ah Peng and begged him for the golden ladle.

"I saw the Dragon King, but he refused to give me anything," he lied. "I am sorry but I cannot help you."

Then he hurried away along the Emperor's Road, weighed down by the heavy pearl in his bag.

A few days later, Ah Shun arrived in the village. As soon as he came to the flood, he pulled out the golden ladle and began to scoop away at the water.

At his first scoop, all the water dried up and the buildings were rebuilt. At the second scoop, all the

crops in the flooded fields grew and ripened. At
the third scoop, the river returned to its normal
banks and flowed peacefully once more.

As the waters receded, a huge oyster shell was
revealed in a muddy field. The mysterious shell
took three strong men to lever open.

Inside, the villagers found an oyster as big and
pink as a giant's tongue. Buried inside its flesh
was a small, black pearl.

The villagers feasted on the oyster, but they insisted that Ah Shun take the black pearl as a reward for saving their village. Ah Shun thanked them and put it in his pocket. He might have failed to find the treasure he sought, but he was glad to have helped to defeat the flood.

After many days of journeying, Ah Peng, the elder brother, arrived back home. Dusk had fallen and the fireflies shone like tiny lanterns. The princess, with her hair still trailing in the river, was waiting for him.

"Did you find a luminous pearl?" she asked.

"I did," replied Ah Peng. "I have it here."

He pulled it out, fully expecting the pearl to light up the night... but nothing happened. The pearl had lost its shine. It sat dull and lifeless in his hands.

The princess gave a tiny shake of her head.

"That is not a luminous pearl," she said gravely.

Overcome with irritation, Ah Peng threw the pearl on the ground. It shattered, releasing a foul-smelling liquid.

Ah Shun arrived home the next morning. When he showed his brother the dull-looking black pearl that he had brought, his brother laughed at him.

"I have seen pebbles that shone more brilliantly than that!" he sneered.

All the same, Ah Shun waited for the princess to appear again that night. She emerged from the water as the sun set. Ah Shun was struck once again by her easy grace and the hint of laughter in her smile.

"I am sorry," he said. "I was unable to find the pearl that you asked for."

"But I can see something in your hand," said the princess. "What is it? Show me."

The Pearl that Shone in the Dark

Ah Shun passed his pearl to the princess,
who threw it up into the sky. Ah Shun
gasped. As it rose higher, the pearl
began to shine a brilliant silver,
lighting up the night like day.

For an instant, it seemed as if two moons hung in the sky. The light was so bright that Ah Shun had to close his eyes. When he opened them again, he was standing inside the Dragon King's underwater palace once more.

The princess was beside him, and both of them were dressed in brilliant crimson and gold robes.

Ah Shun could not hide his confusion. "Who are you really?" he asked. "And what is going on?"

The princess didn't need to reply. When he looked in her eyes, the love that he saw shining there answered all the questions he would ever need to ask. He took her hand gladly.

"Come now," she said, smiling. "Let us go to our wedding."

*This story comes from a very old fable
by a writer named Zhuang Zhi. In China,
the phrase "a frog in a well" is still used to
describe someone ignorant of the wider world.*

The Frog
in the Well

There was once a frog who lived in an old stone well. The walls of the well were crumbling brown stone, coated with soft green moss, and the water was cool and clear. No one used the well any more, so the frog had it all to himself. He had been born in the well, and he lived in the well, and he loved it. It had everything he needed.

The Frog in the Well

He sat all day in a damp, mossy crevice between the stones, waiting for an insect to tumble in. Then – thw-zip! His long pink tongue would whip out and the insect would vanish. There would be a faint crunch, and the frog would smile contentedly. Big juicy flies, clumsy moths, unwary spiders... all kept the frog fat and well-fed.

Occasionally, he wondered if there should be more to life. But, all in all, he wasn't badly off. His particular crevice was so comfortable and gave him a very good view of his world.

The world, the frog knew, was small and ringed with ancient stones, with a calm circle of water below and a neat little circle of blue sky above. Mostly this sky was bright and clear, and the water was as smooth as glass – reflecting the sky so clearly that you might almost forget which was which. But then the sky would grow dull and rain drops would skitter-splatter-splash over the water's surface, shattering the illusion.

Sometimes a sudden gust of wind would send scraps of leaves whirling across the circle of sky or tumbling down to float on the surface of the water before slowly sinking. Very rarely, a head might appear and peer curiously down into the mossy depths before vanishing again. But mostly, what happened was nothing much.

The frog's nights were long and his days were short. It did not take the sun long to travel the little expanse of sky overhead, so he had plenty of time to dream. He dreamed of a bigger world, with broader horizons and longer days, where other frogs croaked by other waters...

Then he would wake, blink slowly at his

familiar surroundings and sigh heavily.

"These are foolish dreams," he told himself. "Look around at the world. You can see how small it is. You know there are no other frogs in it!"

One day, he was sitting in his crevice as usual when something new appeared in his circle of sky. It was the head of a creature, peering down at him with beady black eyes – but it was like no creature he had ever seen before. The frog stared in amazement. It was covered in wrinkly skin and, when it moved, he saw an enormous, domed shell on its back.

The thing nodded at him politely.

"Hello," it called in an old, husky voice.

"Hello," croaked the frog. "What kind of creature are you? And where did you come from? I have never seen anything like you before."

"I am a turtle," it replied. "And my home is the

wide blue ocean. I have swum around the world and visited many places, so if you have not seen me, it is not my fault!"

The frog puffed up its chest. "I don't believe you!" he insisted proudly. "This is the only world and I have never seen you in it."

The turtle chuckled. "If you think this is the only world then you have much to learn, my little

green friend," it said. "Why, this tiny drop of
water is as nothing compared to the ocean. The
ocean has so much water, the greatest flood cannot
fill it and the hottest drought will not dry it up.
Aah the joy, to swim through the foamy waves,
riding the ocean currents – and then to dive down
among the flickering fish, past bright corals and
golden sands."

"You know," the turtle went on, "there are many lands and many seas, and many different kinds of creatures in all of them..."

The frog listened, spellbound, as the turtle described its travels. "Such a large world," he thought in amazement. "I never guessed! I wish I could see it."

Then he looked at his snug little crevice and familiar circle of water and was scared. "What must it be like out there?"

But adventure tugged at him and, slowly but surely, he hopped and crawled from stone to stone, up the sides of the well, up and out...

A cool breeze blew over his damp skin and he shivered with excitement. Then another frog croaked somewhere nearby.

"Just like my dream!" he thought, with a little hop of joy. "I'm not alone after all."

He gazed around at the wide horizon, amazed by the size and variety of everything he saw – trees and grasses and stones and sky and water... and a bright-eyed turtle, watching him.

"Thank you my friend," he told the turtle. "You have opened my eyes. Now I can be an adventurer too!" And with that, he hopped off to explore this thrilling new world.

Chuang Tzu was a legendary Chinese scholar who often expressed his ideas through stories. He wrote this story over 2,000 years ago – and people are still studying its meaning today.

The Butterfly's Dream

The scholar Chuang Tzu lived a simple life. This meant he had less money for food, but more time for thinking. It also meant his clothes were always full of holes and his shoes were tied together with string. All the same, he counted himself amongst the happiest of men.

Because Chuang Tzu had a reputation for seeing to the heart of problems, many people wanted his advice. His fame gradually spread, until the king himself heard of the wise scholar and sent messengers to seek him out. They found the old man fishing on the river, as he often did after lunch.

The messengers jumped off their horses in a cloud of dust, threw themselves to their knees and bowed. Without raising their heads, they offered Chuang Tzu a thousand pieces of silver to come to the capital and advise their king.

"No thanks," said Chuang Tzu. "Now go away. You are scaring the fish."

The fish weren't biting that afternoon, but the weather was warm. Chuang Tzu watched his line and thought about the meaning of life. Soon, his eyes grew heavy and he relaxed into a deep sleep.

The Butterfly's Dream

In his dream, he found himself floating up and
away from his body.

He climbed high above the
river. Surprised by his new
powers, he glanced behind
him and saw that butterfly
wings had sprouted from his
back. The wings were decorated
with bright yellow and blue spots and
fluttered rapidly.

Chuang Tzu looked down at his hands and
saw that they had vanished. In their place, six
spindly legs had sprouted from his furry body.
He realized all at once that he had become
a butterfly.

Instead of being frightened by this strange
turn of events, Chuang Tzu was filled with joy.

The Butterfly's Dream

He flitted here and there, first curving down through the air in a dizzying swoop, then climbing gently up on a gossamer breeze.

New senses unfurled to him. Now, as a butterfly, he could taste the slightest difference in the wind. All the flowers shouted and sang out to him with loud voices, offering up their nectar.

In fact, Chuang Tzu was having such a glorious time that he soon forgot that he had ever been a man. He lost track of time. He had always been a butterfly and nothing else. Life was only this laughing, soaring flutter.

Up so splendid!

Down so wondrous!

It was...

"Chuang Tzu!" A loud voice boomed.

Someone was kicking him.

"Chuang Tzu! The sun is setting. Wake up, old friend."

The wonderful dream crumbled apart like a sandcastle before a wave. Suddenly, Chuang Tzu found himself back on the ground with a knobbly tree at his back and a stiff ache in his neck. He couldn't fly any more.

His friend, Big Chang, was standing over him.

Chuang Tzu blinked slowly. He knew he had lost something amazing, but something else was worrying him too. He looked around at the river and the grass and then up at Big Chang, quite puzzled, as if seeing everything for the first time.

"You look as if you've seen a ghost," said Big Chang. "Come to the inn with me. That'll cheer you up."

Sipping tea at the inn, Chuang Tzu remained lost in thought.

The Butterfly's Dream

"So," said his friend. "It's been ten minutes that you've been sitting here pondering. Why do you still look like someone's turning cartwheels on your grave? A bad dream?"

"Quite the opposite," replied Chuang Tzu. "It was a wonderful dream." And he explained about his joyful time as a butterfly.

"So what's the problem?" asked Big Chang. "That sounds great."

"My problem is that I can't tell if I've woken up or not," replied Chuang Tzu. "This conversation that I'm having with you seems very real. This soothing tea tastes very real too." He took another sip. "But then so did my dream of being a butterfly. That felt just as real... maybe even more."

Big Chang frowned. "I'm not sure that I understand you."

The Butterfly's Dream

Chuang Tzu smiled. "I thought I was Chuang Tzu, dreaming of being a butterfly. But what if I am a butterfly, dreaming of being Chuang Tzu?"

"Bah! What rot!" scoffed Big Chang. "I can assure you that I am very real. So are these delicious almond cakes which I am gobbling. And I can tell that YOU are real, old man, because you are talking nonsense as usual!"

"How can you be so sure?" Chuang Tzu shook his head. "You might be part of my dream. The truth, my friend, is that we have no way of knowing if we're more or less real than anything else."

The two men sat in silence for a bit, contemplating this alarming thought.

The evening was fine. Good smells wafted from the kitchen. More tea came, and skewers of pork, and fried rice and steamed dumplings and many other delicious dishes. The inn was filled with quiet laughter and the clicking of chopsticks.

Big Chang began to feast, stuffing food into his mouth, and smacking his lips.

"Why are you eating so much?" asked Chuang Tzu, after Big Chang had gobbled down his fifth dumpling.

"Well, my friend..." Big Chang grinned through a mouthful of pork. "Maybe you are right. Maybe we are only a butterfly's dream. But if we are, then I reckon it's my duty to make sure that lucky creature's getting the best dream ever!"

There are several versions of this folk tale –
in some, the villain is a wolf, in others, a tiger.
In China, the tale was first written down
by a poet named Huang Zhing.

Great-Aunt Tiger

*O*nce upon a time, Shan and her sisters lived with their mother in a little old house, on the edge of a big old forest. One day, their mother had to go and visit their grandmother. She kissed the girls goodbye and picked up her basket.

"It is a long way and I won't be back until tomorrow," she told them. "So be sure to latch the door at sunset and don't let anyone in."

Great-Aunt Tiger

As the sun was setting, there was a rap on the door. "Open up, my dears," muttered a low, rasping voice. "Your great-aunt has come to visit!"

The girls glanced at each other in surprise.

"Great-aunt?" echoed Shan, puzzled. "But... mother didn't tell us you were coming!"

"She must have forgotten," came the reply. "Now it's getting late. Hurry and let me in!"

The youngest girl, who was standing nearest the door, reached out her hand obediently...

"No, wait," cried Shan, thinking of her mother's warning, but it was too late – her sister had already lifted the latch.

A stooped figure shuffled in, muffled by a huge shawl. Shan peered cautiously through the fading light, but couldn't make out the face.

"Great-aunt, let me take your shawl," she suggested politely.

"No, I'm too cold," grunted the figure, pulling the shawl tighter around itself.

"Great-aunt, what a husky voice you have!" exclaimed Shan.

"Ah, that's my sore throat," sighed the figure.

"Poor Auntie!" exclaimed the youngest, reaching out in sympathy. She withdrew her hand quickly. "Great-aunt, what hairy arms you have!"

"Ah, that's my new fur coat," growled the figure, waving a hand dismissively. Something glinted in the dim light.

"Great-aunt, what long nails you have," said Shan, growing more and more suspicious.

"Ah, I had no time to trim them," snapped the figure impatiently.

Shan was determined to get a better look at their visitor. "It's getting dark," she murmured. "I'd better light a candle..."

"No!" huffed the figure, blowing out the flame. "I prefer the dark."

But in the split second before the flame flickered out, Shan had glimpsed the face beneath the shawl – and it wasn't her great-aunt. It had hungry green eyes, a broad, striped face and a mouth lined with wicked-looking teeth...

"A tiger!" she realized, her heart thumping. "And tigers EAT children. I'll have to get rid of it somehow."

The tiger stared at the girls and licked its lips with a rough red tongue.

"I'm hungry," it rasped. "All I had to eat on the way here was a few fried dough sticks." To demonstrate, the tiger pulled something out of a pocket and crunched it up – though to Shan's sharp glance, it looked more like a bone than a dough stick.

"What's for dinner?" the tiger went on.

Shan thought quickly. "How about fruit?"

"Fruit?" snorted the tiger. "I want meat!"

"Ah, but this is MAGIC fruit," said Shan boldly, winking at her sisters. "It tastes better than anything, even meat! Look, it's growing right there." She pointed to an ancient ginkgo tree outside the window. Round yellow fruit dangled from the topmost twigs.

"I can't climb that high!" complained the tiger.

"That's all right," said Shan, smiling.
"We can climb up and pick some for you."

The tiger hesitated. It didn't want to let the
girls go, but it did want to try the fruit. Then
it had an idea... "All right," it said. "But I
must tie a rope around your waists and hold
one end while you climb."

"Yes Auntie," agreed Shan meekly.

So, roped together like mountaineers, the
three girls climbed up deftly among the tree's
gnarly old branches and fluttering, fan-shaped
leaves. At the top, in a low voice, Shan revealed to
the others what she had seen...

"But it's ok, I have a plan," she went on. "Just
copy me." She reached out a hand and picked some
of the tree's hard yellow fruit.

Her sisters did the same.

"Here's your fruit, Auntie," she called down, taking careful aim...

BAM! BAM! BAM!

Several hard round balls hit the tiger on the end of its nose.

"Ouch," snapped the tiger crossly, rubbing its nose. It eyed the fruit doubtfully. "Are you absolutely sure these things are edible? They're not very soft."

"Well, they should really be cooked," Shan explained. "We can cook them for you, dear Auntie, if you fetch a pot of boiling water."

"Very well," grumbled the tiger. It tied the end of the rope to a nearby post, went into the house and came back with a steaming cooking pot.

The sisters picked more fruit. This time, they aimed at the pot...

SPLISH – SPLOSH – SPLASH!

Scalding hot water fountained up and spattered the tiger's fur.

"O-oh!" it squealed. "Owww! Stop! You're burning me!"

"Sorry Auntie!" called the girls, trying to hide their grins.

"I have a better idea," went on Shan. "Can you tie the end of our rope to the pot? That way, we can pull it up and cook the fruit up here, without splashing you."

"Very well," rumbled the tiger. It took the rope from the post and knotted it around the handles of the cooking pot instead.

The girls heaved and hauled, lifting the heavy pot to the top of the tree. Then Shan balanced it on a branch, while her sisters picked more fruit and pretended to cook it.

"Mmm, that smells delicious," they chorused
loudly, inhaling deeply. "Better than sizzling
steak, better than barbecue pork, even better than
crispy duck..."

Down below, the tiger began to drool.

"Hurry!" it roared.

"Dear Auntie, open your mouth so we can
feed you the cooked fruit," said Shan.

Down below, the greedy tiger opened
his jaws...

WHOOSH!

Shan tipped the whole pot of hot water down
the tiger's throat, while her sisters pelted it with
handfuls of hard fruit.

"Ooow-oooow-ooOOW!" howled the tiger.

That was enough, even for the greediest tiger.
It turned tail and fled deep into the forest, and was
never seen again.

The next day, when their mother got back from their grandmother's house, she praised the girls for their bravery and quick-thinking, and chuckled at the idea of the 'magic' fruit.

"That beast got more than it bargained for when it knocked on our door," she told them proudly. "Foolish creature! I can see, no tiger is going to get the better of you three."

The real 'painter of dragons'
was an artist named Zhang Sengyou,
who lived in China about 1,500 years
ago. His story inspired a saying, "dotting
the dragons' eyes" – meaning to add the
finishing touches.

The Painter of Dragons

It was the end of summer. The old painter Zhang sat as still as a statue, watching red and yellow leaves drift across Nanjing Lake. He had been sitting in the same spot for three days.

On the morning of the fourth day, his assistant approached him nervously.

"Master, I fear the monks grow impatient. They want to know when you will begin the work that they have paid you for."

Zhang made no sign that he had heard, and continued to stare at the water. His assistant, long-used to these silences, sighed and settled down patiently to wait.

After some hours had passed, the old man suddenly spoke in an awed whisper.

"Do you see the dragon?"

Half-asleep, the assistant was alarmed. A huge black dragon was said to dwell in the lake's depths. But when he looked out across the great lake, there was nothing to be seen on the water but ripples and a few carefree ducks. He was a careful man, however, so he did not answer until he had checked the lake thoroughly.

"Master, there is no dragon," he said.

Zhang smiled with the calm that only comes after three days of meditation.

"Is there not?"

He stood up slowly. "You may tell the abbot that I am ready to go to work."

Zhang was an important man. For many years, he had been the Emperor's librarian and also his foremost general, organizing books and armies at the same time. Despite these heavy responsibilities, Zhang's true passion had always remained painting.

His skill with a brush was legendary – especially when it came to painting animals. A decade ago, while holding court in the Summer Palace, the Emperor had been troubled by the loud cooing of doves and pigeons outside his window while he slept. After many solutions had been tried and failed, Zhang solved the problem at a stroke by painting a soaring vulture on one side of the window and a swooping hawk on the other.

Now, the doves and pigeons were frightened

to build their nests nearby, and the Emperor slept in peace.

The abbot of Anle Temple bowed deeply as he greeted Zhang at the temple gate.

"It is a great privilege to have you at our temple, Master Zhang. Now, I was hoping –"

"Yes, yes," interrupted Zhang. "Where are the walls? I want to start on these dragons immediately."

The abbot gave a tiny frown. The usual practice on such an important project was for the artist to make a number of sketches to plan the painting out, and have their assistants prepare the walls. This was all most irregular.

Of course, Zhang understood why the abbot was confused.

"I prepare everything in my mind. Not with the hand," he explained kindly, tapping his finger against his forehead. "What did you think I've been doing these past three days?"

The abbot bowed again and brought Zhang to the chamber he was to decorate.

The artist set to work at once. He painted with great freedom, flying from one wall to the next as the mood took him. On the east wall he painted a dragon in azure blue, and opposite, on the west wall, a dragon in brilliant emerald green. The dragon on the south wall was vermilion red, and the northern beast a deep, midnight black.

A crowd gathered to watch the master at work, peering in through the windows and crowding at the doors. The paintings were truly extraordinary: the dragons' bodies coiled amongst the clouds, as they tossed their horns and clutched at pearls with their great talons. Zhang used remarkably few strokes, but such was his deft touch that the noble

beasts seemed to breathe on the walls.

After a day of furious activity, Zhang Sengyou wiped his hands on his gown, and set his brushes down carefully.

"It is finished," he said.

The monks came in to inspect the work that he had done. As they passed around the room, admiring each of the four dragons, another little frown slowly deepened on the abbot's usually smooth brow.

"Master Zhang," he murmured, after finishing his tour of inspection. "Have you truly finished?"

"Yes, I think so," said Zhang. "Are you not happy with the work?"

"It's the eyes," said the abbot. "You haven't dotted them in." The other monks nodded in agreement – all of the dragons' eyes were white, without pupils. They stared sightlessly from the walls. The effect was a little unnerving.

"Oh, I had no intention of doing that," explained Zhang. "The eyes hold the spirit, you see. If I dot them in, my dragons would come alive and fly off the walls."

The monks consulted together briefly and then returned to Zhang. The abbot made no effort this time to hide his frustration.

"Master Zhang," he said. "With the greatest respect, we would prefer it if we could have four finished dragons – as was stipulated in the contract that you signed and for which we have already paid."

"Are you quite sure of this?" asked Zhang. "It is a bad idea."

"We want our dragons finished," said the abbot. All the monks nodded in agreement

Zhang saw they had made up their minds.

'Just don't say I didn't warn you," he sighed, taking up a pot of black paint. With two quick strokes, he dotted in the eyes of the emerald dragon.

At once, the sky darkened and day turned to night. There was a flash of lightning and a peal of thunder. The plaster on the west wall began to shift and crack.

Unruffled, Zhang dotted in the eyes of the black dragon as well. Now came another lash of lightning, and a wicked wind whirled through the room. The north and west walls bulged as the two dragons wriggled and swelled.

"Stop!" screamed the abbot fearfully, but he was too late.

With a mighty roar, the green and black dragons burst from their walls. Bricks and plaster

flew through the air. Everyone dived for cover as the two great beasts soared up into the air, roaring with delight at their fresh life.

Only Zhang hadn't moved. He watched the two dragons fly away over the lake with the same faint smile he greeted all things, good or bad. The sky quickly went back to normal – but the temple walls would never be the same again. The Abbot looked about him, aghast at the destruction.

"Well," said Zhang. "It's not so bad. At least you still have two dragons left."

In China, the phoenix is a symbol of virtue and grace. The tale of how he came by his beautiful feathers has inspired Chinese painters and musicians for centuries.

How the Phoenix got his Feathers

The phoenix was a gentle, unassuming bird. He lived in the shadows of the forest and, with his drab brown feathers, often went completely unnoticed. He trod so lightly, he left scarcely a footprint behind, and he ate only dewdrops. But when he sang, his song filled the air with breathtaking ripples of sound.

How the Phoenix got his Feathers

The other forest birds paid the phoenix little attention. They spent their days flitting carelessly between the treetops, gossiping and showing off their bright feathers – and gobbling any seeds and berries they found. But if a seed was not quite plump enough, or a berry not quite juicy enough, they would toss it aside. Sometimes they let food fall because they lost interest. Sometimes food dropped because they pecked at it too hastily. The birds didn't care. There was plenty more growing in the forest, so why should they worry?

The discarded seeds and berries tumbled to the forest floor where they lay, unheeded, until the phoenix arrived. From dawn till dusk, this humble brown bird worked tirelessly, collecting up the lost foodstuffs so they would not spoil or go to waste. He carried them to a cave and stored them there carefully, drying the berries and sorting the seeds, until the floor was buried beneath rustling, glimmering heaps.

So life in the forest went on, until one long, hot summer when the rains failed. Day after day, week after week, the sky was a bright, cloudless blue. Seared by unrelenting heat, and lacking any refreshing rain, leaves turned brown, berries withered on the branch and seeds ceased to grow. Before long, there was nothing left to eat and the birds began to despair.

"Hungry, hungry!" chirped a young sparrow.

"Me too," agreed a friendly finch.

"We'll all starve," called a pheasant, rattling its long tail feathers sadly.

"No-no-no food, no food," called the wood pigeons, until the forest echoed with their mournful cries.

Far away, the phoenix heard their lament.

How the Phoenix got his Feathers

"My fellow birds are in trouble," he thought.
"I can help them!" Spreading dull-looking wings,
he took to the air and flew through the trees,
calling out as boldly and bravely as he could: "If
you are in need of food, I have plenty to share.
Follow me and I will show you..."

The other birds flocked eagerly to the call, and
the phoenix led them to his cave. The birds gasped
and chattered excitedly as they flew through the
entrance. Huge mounds of dried berries gleamed
bright as jewels in the dim light, and the mounds
of plump, golden seeds reached almost to the roof.
There would be more than enough to feed every
bird until the rains came again.

"Take whatever you need," said the phoenix.
"There is plenty for everyone, and to spare."
So the birds of the forest were saved
by the kind, hard-working phoenix.

92

How the Phoenix got his Feathers

"Oh wise and far-sighted phoenix, from this day forth you shall be our king!" they cooed and cawed and sang and squawked, raising their voices in joyful celebration.

"Now to show our gratitude, let us give you a gift worthy of royalty," added a wise old magpie.

One by one, each bird stepped forward and plucked a feather out of its own breast or wing or tail, then dropped it onto the floor of the cave. Soon there was a heap of plumes in different shades: pearl white, ebony black, jade green, ruby red and gold. Some of the feathers were speckled, some were striped, and some flashed like fire when they caught the light; all were very beautiful.

Two weaver birds then wove these feathers into a magnificent, many-hued coat and presented it to their new king... and when the phoenix put it on, he was transformed.

No longer a drab brown creature, now he looked truly dazzling. Light shone from his feathers and sparkled in the air around him. His wings gleamed like rainbows and a long, elegant tail spread out behind him.

The phoenix loved his feather coat and wears it to this very day – so if you ever see the king of the birds, you will recognize him at once.

Because of this tale, "there is no silver buried here"
is a famous saying in China. It means that
guilty people give themselves away,
by clumsily claiming to be innocent.

There is No Silver Buried Here

*L*ong, long ago, when there was less noise and more greenery on the banks of the Li River, a poor fisherman named Zhang San went out every night in his leaky old boat. It might seem strange to fish at night, but Zhang was not your usual kind of fisherman; he did not use a net, or a rod and line. Instead he used trained birds known as cormorants.

Cormorant fishing is best done at night, so every evening Zhang lit a lantern and hung it from the prow of his boat. Then, with his clever birds perched beside him, he rowed out into the soft darkness of the river.

When Zhang judged he'd reached a likely spot, he released the cormorants. The flickering light from his lantern lured teeming shoals of river carp – for which the shallow Li River was famed – up to the surface. The cormorants knifed through the water, snapping up fish. The birds gulped the tiddlers down easily enough, but brought the whoppers back to the boat, where Zhang collected them in shivering, silvery piles. In this unusual way, he caught enough carp to sell in the market and provide a modest income.

Zhang was a simple man, but he loved his birds dearly and took very good care of them.

He tried to treat them all equally but, from the moment that he first began working with Kuai, there was only one bird for him. No cormorant had ever learned his craft as quickly as Kuai did, nor had any bird ever had such a wise and understanding eye.

"We will go far together Kuai, you and I," said Zhang, the first time he took Kuai fishing.

It might seem crazy to talk to a bird, but on those long, lonely nights on the river, Zhang used

to have long conversations with his cormorants.

In any case, Zhang was right: Kuai was a masterful fisher. He caught five times as many fish as the rest of the birds put together. Very soon, the few copper coins that Zhang took home every morning from the market became silver coins instead. This had never happened before.

At first Zhang was delighted at his newfound wealth, but soon he began to worry.

"I spend all night on the river," he said to Kuai. "But what if someone steals my money while I'm away? I can't take the coins with me, because they would weigh down the boat – but I can't spend them all at once either." This was true. Zhang was a man of very simple tastes.

Kuai didn't answer but dived into the black water. A few seconds later he emerged, proudly, with yet another fat carp lodged in his throat.

As the silver piled up, Zhang's money worries grew more troubling. Soon he had more than three hundred silver pieces sitting in a box under his bed. Fear kept him from sleeping.

After a few months he had grown pale and tired, worn out by his dilemma.

"My friend, Wang Er the pig farmer, made a suspicious remark today," said Zhang as he rowed out onto the river. "He wondered what I was planning to do with all the money I was saving."

Kuai, sitting on the edge of the boat, seemed to shake his head in a world-weary fashion.

"I quite agree, Kuai," said Zhang. "Wang Er can be greedy. The temptation of my money might be too much for him. You are right; I must do something about the money soon."

Watching the bird carefully, Zhang thought he saw Kuai nod in agreement.

On the river, Zhang was an expert. He knew every current and rock, the mood of the fish, and how things changed with the weather and the seasons. But away from the water, it was another story. Zhang was about as at home on dry land as a carp in the desert and he was uncomfortably aware of this. So he knew he needed to be especially careful how he stored his money.

Early the next morning, after he had put his cormorants in the shed where they roosted, he snuck out into his garden and dug a deep hole beneath a cherry tree. Then he buried his box of silver coins as quickly as he could, hoping that Wang Er wasn't watching.

Just to be on the safe side, he added one final cunning touch. Taking a piece of wood, he wrote on it: "Three hundred pieces of silver are NOT buried here." and nailed it to the trunk of the tree.

Thoroughly satisfied with his morning's work, Zhang went to bed and dreamed his first untroubled dream in months. When he awoke towards sunset, he went outside to check that all was well.

He was horrified to see the ground beneath the cherry tree had been dug up and his box of silver was gone. Written on the tree was a new line: "Wang Er did NOT steal three hundred coins."

For the rest of the chilly night, rowing along the river with his birds, Zhang was both distraught and terribly puzzled. He tried to work out who had stolen his money by talking to Kuai. "Wang Er would have been the first man I suspected," he said. "But it is quite clear that he is innocent. The sign told me as much. I wonder which rogue has taken them?"

Kuai fixed Zhang with that quizzical bird look, which seemed to say that the world was strange and vast and filled with untold mysteries.

"I know, Kuai, I know," said Zhang. "You birds are much better than people."

The fishing was not good that night, and Zhang returned to his mooring an unhappy man. He was surprised to discover Wang Er waiting for him on the bank.

"That's funny," said Zhang to himself. "What can he want?"

"Good morning, Zhang!" said Wang. "I have a surprise for you." From behind his back he produced the stolen box of silver.

"Incredible!" cried Zhang, delighted. "But tell me, how did you catch the thief?"

"You are surprised." Wang Er blinked, utterly astonished. "Did you not guess who had taken it?

He left you a big clue."

"I have no idea," said Zhang. "It is a great mystery to me – and I still can't fathom how the rogue knew where to dig, either. How on earth did you catch him?"

"How did I catch him?" Wang Er began to chuckle, then to laugh and then his laughter turned to uncontrollable roars of amusement. With his body shaking, he had to sit down on the bank to recover.

Zhang and the cormorants watched this display with amazement.

"He is quite crazy, because he spends all his time with pigs," whispered Zhang to Kuai. "But I am grateful to the fellow, so I will not tell anyone he has lost his wits."

He waited patiently for Wang Er to stop laughing. "You were going to tell me how you caught the thief," he said when his friend had regained his composure.

"I... It was a struggle," said Wang Er, fighting off another wild attack of the chuckles. "I... I had to look deep inside myself to find the truth." He giggled again. "I searched far and wide, but the answer was right there, staring me in the face all along. To catch the culprit, all I had to do was look in the mirror."

"In the mirror?" said Zhang. "So you found him with magic? That's very clever."

Wang looked up at Zhang with a look of complete amazement on his face "My friend... I do know the thief was trying to help you."

"He was?" said Zhang. "Stealing a man's silver is a strange way to go about helping. It seems to me that the only person helping me was you, Wang Er."

"That's because I was the thief," said Wang Er with a defeated sigh.

"You?" Zhang's mouth gaped wide like one of his carp. "But... but..."

Wang Er patiently waited for his friend to work it all out. This took some time. He watched a number of expressions pass across Zhang's face – bafflement, puzzlement, wonderment and, at last, a smile.

"So you did it to help me," said Zhang. "Hah!
I understand everything now!"

"I hope so." Wang Er got up and put his arm
around Zhang's shoulders. "Now, my friend,
would you like some breakfast?"

As the sun rose above the misty river, the two
men tied up the boat and carried the box of money
back to Zhang's house.

Versions of this folk tale are told across China and Asia. Even today, some people leave out food for mice on the third day of the Chinese New Year – the day of the 'Mouse Marriage'.

The Mouse's Marriage

O nce upon a time, there was a family of
mice: a mother mouse, a father mouse
and their only child – a clever little girl
mouse, with soft white fur, dainty paws and
a slender pink tail. Her parents adored her
and tried to give her the best of everything,
from the fattest bacon rinds to the softest
scraps of bedding.

The family lived together quietly but happily, until the daughter was old enough to start her own family. "It is time our dear daughter was married," the mother mouse told the father one day.

"We must find her the very best husband," said the father. "Someone strong and powerful."

"Yes," said the mother. "So he will always be able to take care of our darling. Who is the strongest creature in all the world?"

The father mouse wrinkled his nose in thought, watching a golden ray of sunlight steal slowly across the floor of the mousehole... "I know," he squeaked suddenly. "The Sun! There is no one more mighty, for his rays warm the whole world."

The mother nodded and called their daughter. Together, the family scampered up to the top of a hill. It was a clear spring day. Overhead, the sun was shining brightly.

The Mouse's Marriage

The father mouse sat up on his haunches and called up, "Oh Sun, are you the greatest creature in all the world?"

The sun smiled and shone even more brightly. But before it could answer, a soft breeze stirred the air, sending a little white cloud scudding in front of the sun's face.

"Look," said the mouse mother, as the sun's light was dimmed. "The cloud is mightier than the sun! See how it stops the sun's rays."

So the mouse father called up, "Oh Cloud, are you the greatest creature in all the world?"

The cloud puffed up with pride. But before it could answer, the breeze began to blow harder – breaking the cloud into little white wisps.

"Look," said the mouse mother. "The wind is mightier than the cloud! See how easily it blew the cloud apart."

So the mouse father called again, "Oh Wind, are you the greatest creature in all the world?"

The wind blew a great gust of delight. It blew with such force, it tumbled the little mice right off the top of the hill. Head over heels they rolled, bumping and thumping...

"Eeee," squealed the mice. "Ooo-ow!"

BUMP! Their wind-blown fall was halted by an old, stone wall. Gratefully they staggered to their feet and smoothed their fur.

"Well," said the mouse mother. "This wall is mightier than the wind! See how easily it stopped that gust."

The mouse father nodded. "Oh Wall," he said. "Are you the greatest creature in the world?"

The wall said nothing, being only a wall – but as the mice waited for an answer, they heard something scrabbling nearby.

"What's that?" wondered the mother.

"Look!" squeaked the daughter, pointing.

There, near the foot of the wall, was a little hole. As they watched, a flurry of dust flew out of it – followed by a whiskery face. It was another mouse, digging and scraping a hole to live in.

"THERE is the mightiest creature in the world," said the mouse daughter, smiling. "See how easily he makes a hole in the wall! I should marry a mouse." Her mother and father had to agree – the proof was there before their pointy pink noses. So a little while later, the mouse daughter married a mouse husband; in fact, the same mouse they had met making the hole in the wall.

He was a handsome black mouse, with very sleek whiskers and a very kind heart, and he was delighted to find a wife to share his snug new home in the wall.

All the mice came from miles around to celebrate the marriage with singing and dancing. They brought gifts of biscuits and bacon rinds, and held a great feast by the light of the new spring moon.

The wedding day was the third day of the Chinese New Year – and some people in China still say that if you stay out late on that day, you might meet a crowd of mice celebrating. But it is best to go to bed early, so as not to disturb them, and to leave out some food, so the mice will be happy and not make any mousey mischief in the year to come.

This story first
appeared in an ancient book
of philosophy known as the "Liezi."
It was repeated by Chinese leader
Mao Zedong, in a famous speech in 1945.

The Old Man who Moved a Mountain

*I*n times long past, an old man named
Yu Gong lived in the shade of two tall
mountains. He was so old he had forgotten
his actual age, but he had lived a long and
happy life. To his great delight he had six
strong sons and seven sturdy daughters,
an army of grandchildren and great
grandchildren, and a wife who loved
him, even though he had snored every
night without fail for sixty years.

The Old Man who Moved a Mountain

Like many in his village, Yu Gong was a fisherman. He woke every morning in total darkness because the two mountains blocked the light from the rising sun. Along with the rest of the fishermen, he then trudged for an hour to get to his boat. The walk took so long because everyone had to circle around the mountains to reach the sea. In the evening, laden down with fish, it took even longer.

Over many years, Yu Gong had developed an intense dislike for those awkward mountains. They were a blot on his otherwise blessed existence, a daily irritation, a dark cloud in the sunny sky of his life.

One evening, after yet another backbreaking march, Yu Gong suddenly realized that he couldn't take it any longer. Arriving home, he threw down his basket of fish in dramatic fashion.

"My family! Come and listen!" he shouted.
"I have something important to tell you!"

Many of his children and grandchildren lived
in houses nearby, and they all gathered to hear
what Grandfather had to say. Even the swarms of
great-grandchildren sensed that something big
was happening. They listened quietly, clutching
their parents' hands.

"My family! I am not going fishing tomorrow,"
Yu Gong announced. "I've had enough!"

"Are you retiring at last?" called his wife, Lu
Hua. "It's about time, old man."

"Far from it, virtuous wife," said Yu Gong.
"I have a new plan. I intend to get rid of those
pesky mountains!"

"You... are going to do what now, husband?"
Lu Hua sat down, blinking in astonishment.
Various daughters rushed over to attend her.

"Wife, I am going to dig." Yu Gong smoothed his beard, which had become ruffled in his excitement. "I've had a vision! I want to clear the way to the boats! Don't you see?" He pointed up at the mountains that loomed balefully over the village. "If we shift those two hummocks, it will only take us a few minutes to stroll to the sea. Think of all the time we will save."

"What a fine idea!" cried his children, who were just as sick of the mountains as their father. "An excellent plan! When do we start?"

"Eee! You've all gone mad!" said Lu Hua, hissing like a frustrated kettle. "Look at you, husband! Your arms are as thin as birch twigs. You complain about your back every time I ask you to sweep the floor. You are so old, you can barely lift a pig. How are you going to move one mountain, let alone two?"

"My family will help me," said Yu Gong
simply. "We start tomorrow."

The family rose at dawn. Yu Gong attacked
the mountain first, but anyone who could be
spared from their usual jobs joined the dig:
fathers, daughters, cousins, sons, even the
tiny children helped out, carrying soil
and roots away in baskets on
their backs.

After one day the family had dug a small hole; after three days it was certainly bigger; after a week, it might even have been described as deep. But neither Yu Gong nor his family were downhearted at this crawling progress. They continued to chip away, day by day. Steadily, slowly, their hole grew.

Meanwhile the two mountains towered above them, utterly indifferent to the tiny ants scratching away at their toes.

Other villagers came to see the bizarre spectacle. At first, utterly baffled, they simply stared. But after two weeks had passed and the family still showed no sign of giving up, their bafflement turned to mockery.

"Yu Gong!" called one old woman, leaning over the edge of the hole. "You are older than a turtle! But even if you lived another ten turtle lives, you will never finish this task!"

"Look at those mountains!" cried a fellow fisherman. "They are laughing at you."

Yu Gong continued digging. His family, following his example, ignored the jeering and kept on digging too.

"There are easier things to do with your old age than dig up a mountain," said an old man named Zhi Sou, who thought himself very wise. "Why not play chess? Or take up calligraphy? Think of your back! Think of your wife!"

This last provocation Yu Gong could not stand. He turned to face the man.

"Old man," he said. "You do not understand something as obvious as that large nose on your face. You are more foolish than the youngest of my great-grandchildren."

"Nonsense!" Zhi Sou sniffed. "Yu Gong, you

have embarrassed yourself and your family. You are a disgrace to this village."

"You are right that I am old," replied Yu Gong. "And it is certain that I will die before we can move these mountains. But a disgrace? I think not." He pointed at his many helpers. "Look at my family here. Look at my brave, strong-backed sons and daughters, my grandchildren and great-grandchildren. Think of the many generations that haven't even been born yet!"

"Hear this!" Now Yu Gong turned and shouted a challenge up at the mountains themselves. "My family will live on long after I am gone! You may be big, but you are not going to grow any bigger. If we continue our work, I know that one day we will beat you and clear a path all the way to the sea!"

Yu Gong's family cheered his speech and then carried on patiently digging. Zhi Sou was silenced – what could he say in the face of such determination?

He wasn't the only person who'd heard Yu Gong's challenge with keen interest. It so happened that an immortal spirit had made its home high up on one of the forested peaks. At first the spirit had laughed at the tiny people beetling away at the foot of its mountain – but now it began to worry about what might happen to its home.

"Yu Gong is right," thought the spirit. "If his family continues the work, then one day, as he predicts, they will demolish the mountain and I will lose my house."

In great distress, the immortal spirit flew up to Heaven and petitioned the Jade Emperor, the ruler of Heaven, for an audience.

"There is an old man with an iron will digging up my mountain. His family have vowed to finish his task, even if he dies. They are unstoppable. You have to do something!"

The Jade Emperor listened with interest to the spirit's story, sipping a soothing tea.

"It seems to me that this man is admirable," said the Jade Emperor thoughtfully. "His family's sense of duty is without fault. They are hard-working and devoted. This family is worthy of the greatest respect."

"But my mountain, my lord!" pleaded the distraught spirit. "My mountain!"

The Jade Emperor considered the matter.

He took two more sips of tea, before nodding his head firmly.

"Good spirit," said the Jade Emperor. "I have made my judgement. Let us see if there isn't something that can be done."

The next morning, Yu Gong woke up early with bright sunshine streaming into his bedroom from outside. This had never happened before in his life.

Shouting his wife awake, he ran across to the window. What he saw made him fall to his knees in astonishment.

Ever since he was born, the two mountains that towered to the east of the village had blocked out the light of the morning sun. But this morning they were nowhere to be seen. Overnight, someone had picked up the mountains and moved them.

Yu Gong and the rest of his village now had a
clear, uninterrupted view of the morning sun rising
over the East China Sea.

"I've never seen anything so beautiful in my
life," said Yu Gong.

He strolled out into the morning and down
to the beach. Just as he had predicted, it took no
time at all.

Yu Gong gave a deep, satisfied sigh.

The glittering waves murmured on the pebbles,
and a few seagulls bobbed on the water, snacking
on shrimp. It was going to be a glorious day.

This story comes from a collection
of tales by Duan Chengshi, written over
1,000 years ago during the Tang Dynasty.

The Golden Slippers

Once, long ago, there lived a chieftain's daughter named Yeh Shen. Her mother and father had died, and she lived with her stepmother and stepsister. Yeh Shen had hair as black as raven feathers and eyes as green as jade. She was as beautiful as her stepsister, Jun Li, was plain – and her stepmother and stepsister scowled with jealousy whenever they saw her.

The Golden Slippers

Out of spite, they treated Yeh Shen like a servant, and Yeh Shen was too kind and gentle to complain. She spent her days sweeping floors and scrubbing pots, making beds and mending clothes, clearing weeds and carrying heavy cans of water, until she ached all over with tiredness.

In return, her stepmother gave her the scruffiest old clothes and the smallest bowls of rice, so she was often hungry. Sometimes, when her work was done, she would take a few scraps of food, wrap herself in a tattered old cloak and escape down to the river for a little while.

One day, while she sat on the bank, she glimpsed a flash of gold beneath the rippling water. She leaned over for a closer look – and saw a large, golden fish staring up at her and fluttering its fins, almost as if it were waving to her.

"Hello," said Yeh Shen. "Are you hungry too?"

The Golden Slippers

She had a crust of bread with her, so she crumbled it over the river. The fish poked its head out of the water to gulp down the crumbs. It looked so friendly, Yeh Shen began to talk to it. She told it about her life, about how she could never please her stepmother, no matter how hard she tried, and how much she missed her real mother and father. The fish gazed at her as if it understood – and Yeh Shen felt a little less lonely.

After that, Yeh Shen began to visit the river every day.

The Golden Slippers

Every day, the fish came, and she shared her food and her sorrows with it.

Yeh Shen's frequent absences made her stepsister curious. So, secretly, she followed Yeh Shen down to the river and watched her scatter crumbs. When the golden fish appeared, she gasped and ran home to tell her mother.

"Ma, you'll never guess what Yeh Shen is doing. She's feeding our bread to a fish in the river – and talking to it!"

"A fish?" said her mother, licking her lips. "Mm, I like a bit of fish." And she made a plan.

Next day, while Yeh Shen was busy cleaning the house, her stepmother put on the tattered cloak, walked to the river and threw out a fistful of crumbs. Unsuspecting, the golden fish put its head out of the water as usual – and she grabbed it. The fish twisted and turned, trying to get away. Its golden scales were wet and slippery, but she held on tight and reached for her knife to finish it off...

Once it had stopped moving, she picked it up to carry home. "This will make a good meal," she gloated, feeling its weight in her arms.

When she got home, she tossed the fish down on the kitchen table. "Look what I caught," she announced carelessly, as Yeh Shen came in.

Yeh Shen took one glance and ran out of the house, sobbing into her sleeve. She ran all the way to the river and threw herself down on the bank.

"Oh fish, I'm so sorry," she wept miserably. "I wish you were still here."

"Take comfort," came an unfamiliar voice. "All is not lost." Yeh Shen looked up, astonished. She was sure she had been alone on the bank, but now an old man dressed in a shimmering white robe, with long, white hair, was standing before her.

The Golden Slippers

"That was no ordinary fish," he continued. "It was a magical creature, and the magic lives on in its bones. Keep them, and they will help you when you truly need it."

Yeh Shen swallowed hard and nodded.

"Thank you," she whispered. Her eyes were blurred with tears, so she rubbed them. When she looked again, the man was gone. "He must have been magic too," she told herself. "I'd better hurry back so I can get the bones before they're thrown away."

By the time she reached home, her stepmother and stepsister had eaten the whole fish. They were sitting, carelessly sipping tea, at a table littered with dirty bowls and plates.

"How dare you run off like that?" snapped her stepmother crossly. "Well, you missed dinner, so there won't be any food for you tonight! Now, hurry up and clean these dishes."

Yeh Shen took the dishes outside, fetched a pail of water and began to wash up. When no one was looking, she carefully washed the delicate ivory fishbones, too. Then she gathered the bones into an old clay pot and hid them under her bed.

Months passed and the seasons changed, until it was time to celebrate the Spring Festival. This was an important holiday and the whole village buzzed with excitement. Outside, red silk lanterns trimmed with golden tassels were strung along the streets, and red paper decorations were pasted on the windows and doors of all the houses. Inside, the rooms were swept spick and span, and pots of steaming dumplings simmered on stoves, ready for the evening's feast.

Later on, there would be music mixed with the pop and crackle of firecrackers. Fireworks would light up the night with fizzing flashes and showers of stars – and all the young folk would go out to watch, dressed in their finest clothes, hoping perhaps to meet a future husband or wife.

Jun Li had a brand new outfit especially for the occasion, all padded red satin and fancy gold trim. It made her look like a round, red tomato, but her mother fussed over her as if she were the most beautiful girl in the world.

"You look lovely," she said, combing out her daughter's lank hair and pinning it up with combs and a large red satin bow. 'Just like me at your age! All the young men will want to talk to you."

"Please stepmother, may I go out tonight too?"

begged Yeh Shen. "I'll finish all my chores first,
I promise!"

"You?" sneered her stepmother. "No one
wants to see you – and you can't go out in those
rags! No, you'll have to stay at home."

So when she and Jun Li swept out to join the
celebrations, in a swish of satin and a jangle of
bangles, Yeh Shen was left behind.

"Oh, I wish I could go and watch the
fireworks," she sighed. Then, she remembered the
old man's words. "Perhaps I can! I wonder..."

She ran up to the attic where she slept and
reached under her bed for the pot. Clutching the
pot in her hands and squeezing her eyes tightly
shut, she wished as hard as she could.

"Dear fish, please will you help me go to the
Spring Festival?" Then she held her breath and
waited hopefully... but she heard and felt nothing.

The Golden Slippers

Refusing to give up hope, she waited a little longer. Still nothing.

Sadly, she opened her eyes – and gasped.

Instead of her rags, she was now wearing a magnificent gown of soft blue silk, with long, flowing sleeves and a broad, embroidered sash. When she moved, the silk rippled and shimmered, like the river in summer sunshine.

Around her shoulders nestled a cape of brilliant blue kingfisher feathers. Delicate gold and turquoise combs pinned back her long, raven-black hair. Most magical of all, on her feet were two tiny golden slippers, embroidered all over with a pattern of sparkling fish scales.

Hardly daring to believe it, she took a step and then another... she felt as if she were walking on air. She spun around in joy and the dress swirled softly around her, like water.

The Golden Slippers

"It's wonderful," she whispered happily. "Oh, thank you, fish!"

When Yeh Shen arrived at the festival, her appearance drew many astonished and admiring glances, but no one recognized the girl wearing the magical dress. She wandered through the crowd, soaking up the atmosphere, thrilled to be part of the celebrations. A few of the bolder villagers asked her name, and where she came from. In answer, she only smiled and shook her head, afraid to reply in case her stepmother heard about it.

In the distance, she heard the whizz of a rocket. Then, with a loud bang, a fiery flower bloomed overhead – and another, and another. The fireworks had begun. Everyone stopped talking and turned their gaze upwards, ooh-ing and aah-ing.

Yeh Shen was watching, dazzled by the display, when she felt a touch on her arm. Startled, she glanced around and found herself face-to-face with her stepsister.

Jun Li was staring at the beautiful stranger with open curiosity.

"Who are you?" she demanded. "I like your clothes. I must ask mother for a blue dress. You know, you look very like my stepsister Yeh Shen! I wonder if we could be related..."

Terrified she was about to be discovered, Yeh Shen dodged back into the crowds. As she raced through the dark streets she stumbled, leaving one golden slipper on the ground behind her. She didn't dare pause to pick it up.

By the time she reached home, her beautiful blue gown had turned back to rags. Her bare foot was muddy and numb with cold, but her other foot felt warm and dry... She glanced down and saw a glint of gold beneath her tattered tunic.

The Golden Slippers

The other slipper was still there! Yeh Shen smiled to herself as she took it off.

"That was a magical evening," she sighed, as she hid it carefully beside the pot of bones. Meanwhile, the other slipper lay lost in the dark.

Very early the next morning, a merchant came through Yeh Shen's village, on his way to the royal palace with a cartload of candied plums.

As the sun rose in the sky, the merchant saw something sparkling on the road ahead.

"What's that?" he wondered, stopping to take a closer look. He found himself holding a tiny golden slipper, embroidered all over with fish scales. "Amazing," he sighed, turning it over and over in his hands. "The thread must be pure gold!"

The slipper seemed so beautiful, so rare and unusual, that he decided to present it as a gift to the king when he reached the palace.

The Golden Slippers

The king, when he saw it, was just as intrigued. "It's beautiful," he said. "So tiny, and such embroidery... I've never seen anything like it. I wish I could meet the woman who wore it!"

Determined to find her, he sent troops of soldiers out to search for her. They rode far and wide, checking every town and village. Yeh Shen was outside watering vegetables when a troop came clattering through her village. Seeing their royal uniforms, she stopped and bowed politely – but the soldiers scarcely noticed. They thought they were looking for a fine lady, not a ragged servant girl, and rode on without stopping.

After many days and nights, the soldiers returned to the king, shaking their heads. "We are sorry, but we cannot find her," they said.

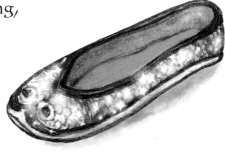

The Golden Slippers

Still the king did not give up. "Put the slipper in a pavilion where all may see it," he said. "Then, let it be known that I wish to return this treasure to its rightful owner – if she can show it fits her foot."

As news of the king's declaration spread, many women came to see the tiny slipper. They waited for hours to try it on, but it was always too small for them. So it remained in the pavilion, under the watchful eye of the king's guards.

Very late one evening, after the other women had all gone home, a slender figure appeared out of the darkness. Yeh Shen had heard about the slipper in the pavilion, and had come to see if it was hers. She had walked for miles and mud spattered her shabby clothes. She recognized the slipper at once. But as her fingers closed around it, another hand seized hers. It was one of the guards.

The Golden Slippers

"Hey!" he said gruffly. "What are you doing? Trying to steal this valuable slipper, no doubt."

"I'm not a thief!" exclaimed Yeh Shen. "That slipper belongs to me. Please, I can prove it – if you will just let me try it on…"

The guard did not listen. He was sure the slipper could not belong to such a ragamuffin. So he arrested her and dragged her before the king.

When he saw them, the king's face darkened. "What are you doing?" he thundered. "Let this lady go at once!"

"But your majesty, she tried to steal the golden slipper!" protested the guard.

The king shook his head. Despite the rags, he had seen at once that this was no ordinary girl.

"Please, accept my apologies for the way my guard has treated you," he told Yeh Shen gently. He glanced at the slipper, still clutched in her trembling hand. "Will you try it?"

Yeh Shen nodded. She reached down and slipped it onto her foot – and it was a perfect fit!

The king gazed deep into her jade-green eyes and smiled. "I have searched the country for you," he said. "I am very glad to have found you at last."

"No – it must be a trick!" insisted the guard. In reply, Yeh Shen reached into a pocket and pulled out something glittering... the other slipper.

As she put it on, her rags were transformed into

a dazzling blue dress, with silken folds that fell like water. A cape of kingfisher feathers nestled on her shoulders and gold combs gleamed in her raven hair. Everyone gasped, able at last to see what the king already knew – that here was a true queen.

"Let no one have any more doubts," declared the king loudly. He turned to Yeh Shen and bowed low. "My lady, may I ask you to be my queen… that is, will you marry me?"

"Yes," whispered Yeh Shen softly, her heart swelling with unaccustomed joy. "I will."

And so Yeh Shen and the king were married. When the king heard about her cruel stepmother and stepsister, he had them banished from the kingdom. But Yeh Shen and the king lived long and happily – thanks to the magical golden fish and the embroidered golden slippers.

The Monkey King is one of China's most beloved
mythical characters. Many stories about him,
including this one, were collected by Wu Cheng'en,
in the book "Journey to the West."

The Monkey King

Once upon a time, back when the world was young, a rock sat on the side of a mountain. The mountain was called Flower Fruit Mountain and it loomed over a small island far to the west of the world of men. The rock was very ordinary. It wasn't big or covered in interesting moss and no one had come to visit it for thousands of years.

So far so quiet, except that the universe, slow and patient as a tortoise, was hatching a secret plan. As the seasons whizzed by, this very ordinary rock was baked by the sun and flaked by the snow, caressed by the moon and tickled by the wind. As the years passed it changed shape, gradually coming to look more and more like a monkey. At last, the resemblance became so uncanny that the stone monkey couldn't help but spring miraculously to life.

"Ho!" cried Monkey, hopping about with glee. "Let's have some fun!"

For a glorious innocent time, that's just what Monkey did. He soon made friends with the other, ordinary monkeys who lived on the island. He chomped fruits and nuts, and bounced through the high treetops. He played crafty tricks and told silly jokes. Sometimes he had naps that lasted for three whole days.

But this Monkey was destined
for greater things. Climbing beside a
waterfall one day, he dived – just for the
sheer splash-smashing joy of it – through the
roaring curtain of water. In the dank darkness
behind the waterfall, he made an astonishing
discovery: a flower-filled cave, lined with houses
carved from stone.

"This is paradise!" he cackled, hopping about
with glee. "I will call it the Cave of the
Waterfall."

Naturally, he invited all the other monkeys to
come and live there with him. Once these
monkeys had settled in, they were so delighted
with their new home that they decided to make
Monkey their king.

For hundreds of years all was well in this

happy little kingdom, until the day Monkey began to think about the future. Suddenly he was overwhelmed by thoughts of death and started weeping.

"Why are you sad, my Lord?" asked the other monkeys, much concerned.

"It's no good! These fun little games we play don't matter," Monkey explained. "In the end we all die, and Lord Yama, the Lord of the Underworld, has the last laugh."

One of the monkeys then told him about some humans who had learned the secret of immortality and the art of NOT dying.

"Melon-head!" said Monkey. "Why didn't you mention this useful skill to your king before? Well, I will soon steal all their secrets, just you watch."

Without pausing for breath, Monkey built himself a raft and sailed across the ocean to the world of men. There, he wandered about the cities, villages and hamlets asking everyone he met if they knew how to live forever. He found no one who did. Humans only seemed to care about boring things like the price of rice or breeding the fattest ox. Monkey found them all rather dull.

At last, after several years of searching, someone suggested he visit the cave of an ancient holy man named Subhodi. Monkey hopped over there as fast as he could.

He found an old, wizened gentleman sitting outside the cave sipping tea.

"Who are you?" Subhodi looked Monkey up and down. "WHAT are you, in fact?"

"I am the Monkey King, you old wrinkleface, and I've been hunting for someone with a bit of sense for a very long time. Now, tell me how to live forever!"

Subhodi had indeed lived a long time – and in all his many years he'd never met a creature quite this cheeky – but he was wise enough to see that Monkey showed promise.

"Study with me," he replied. "And maybe you'll learn."

At first, Monkey had to sweep the floor and make the beds of the other students. But he worked so hard that Subhodi soon began to teach him real magic. Monkey grew faster and stronger, and learned the delightful art of somersaulting through the clouds for thousands of miles in any direction. He discovered the secret magic words that let him change his shape into any of seventy-two forms, and a spell that allowed him to grow as large as a mountain, or as small as a cricket.

These new powers eventually got Monkey into trouble. Teased by the other students, who wanted

to see a good trick, Monkey changed himself into
a towering pine tree. When Subhodi heard their
laughter, he was furious.

"Insolent monkey!" he barked. "You think I've
taught you these holy secrets just so you can show
off? I will NEVER teach you the secret of
immortality. Leave at once!"

Shaking pine needles out of his fur, Monkey

returned home to the Cave of the Waterfall, twenty years after he had left it.

The trip went much quicker this time, because he could somersault across the clouds. But he didn't get the warm welcome he was expecting. Instead of a feast, all his monkey subjects were lurking about in the forest, looking scrawny and disgruntled.

"Where've you been all these years?" they complained. "A three-headed monster called the Demon of Havoc has taken over our cave. He's fatter than ten elephants and he eats monkeys for breakfast!"

"Aha!" said Monkey. "Let's see if this demon likes Monkey fist for lunch."

He marched up to the waterfall. "Hey dog breath!" he bellowed, roaring louder than the waterfall. "I've got a bone to pick with you!"

When the Demon of Havoc stuck his three heads through the wall of water, Monkey charged straight in. He walloped the monster so hard, he smashed one head into Monday, another into Tuesday and the third all the way into Friday afternoon.

Even Monkey was a little awestruck by how strong he was now. No sooner had this thought occurred to him than he wanted to take things further. "Imagine if I had a weapon instead of just my fists," he thought. "That demon would have ended up in a different year!"

There was only one place to go. The Dragon King of the Eastern Sea was famous for the wonders and weapons in his treasure house.

A short while later, the Dragon King was sitting down to tea when he heard a thunderous banging and clanging on his palace doors.

"There's a tough-looking monkey outside,"
reported a lobster guardsman. "He demands to see
you, your majesty. He says he's a king."

"A monkey king?" said the Dragon King,
raising an exquisite eyebrow. "How tough can a
monkey be? Well, show him in!"

"What's up, chief?" said Monkey, swaggering
in. He slouched into a chair and made himself
thoroughly at home. The Dragon King decided to
overlook this appalling lack of manners.

"To what do I owe the pleasure of this visit, O
Monkey King?" he asked politely.

Now Monkey was grabbing handfuls of
pastries and stuffing them in his mouth. "Mmm-
yum! I need a weapon, so I can defend my people,"
explained Monkey, still chewing. "I'm asking for a
kindness, see? King to king."

The Dragon King liked to be generous, so he

ordered ten eel attendants to carry out a famous
great sword. It weighed over a ton – but Monkey
swished it about as if it was nothing, before
tossing it away.

"Far too flimsy!" he scoffed.

Beneath his emerald scales, the Dragon King
turned pale with fear. "This monkey is truly a
dangerous creature!" he breathed to himself.

"What about that little thing over there?" said
Monkey, pointing to the enormous iron pillar that
held up the roof. It stood as tall as a tree in the
middle of the room.

"Are you joking?" gasped the Dragon King.
"That's the magic iron pillar which pounded the
Milky Way flat, when the stars were first forged.
It's far too heavy to move."

"Oh really?" said Monkey. He strolled over
and picked up the pillar as easily as if it were a

broomstick. "Though you're right, this pillar is a little awkwardly sized."

Immediately, the giant pillar shrank until it was the size of an actual broomstick. The Dragon King shivered.

"A bit smaller, I think," said Monkey. The iron rod shrank to the size of a matchstick. Monkey popped it behind his ear.

"Now that's what I call a weapon!" he grinned. "But chief, I have some other requests..."

The Dragon King didn't dare to refuse. He gave Monkey everything he asked for –

even summoning his brother dragons, who brought
Monkey flying shoes, a hat with a phoenix feather
plume and a golden breastplate.

Monkey was delighted with his loot and
returned to his monkeys in triumph. That evening,
after a raucous celebratory feast, he went to sleep
fully dressed – still wearing his presents of course.

In his dreams, he was rudely seized by two
grim-faced demons. They threw a rope around him
and dragged his soul down to the Land of the
Dead, the underworld kingdom ruled over by
Lord Yama.

"Your time is up, dead Monkey," they sneered.
"You are Lord Yama's now."

Back in the real world, Monkey
had stopped breathing – but in the Land of the
Dead, he was still alive and very angry. Quick as
a flash, he pulled the iron pillar from behind his ear

and blew on it. As soon as it was a good size, he thwacked the two demons upside down and raced off. Demons fled before him, in terror of this furry whirlwind of pain.

Dismayed by the uproar in his kingdom, Lord Yama sent the ten judges of the Courts of Death to intercept Monkey. They tried to calm him down, but he was having none of it.

"You see, your name is written down in the Book of the Dead," the judges explained. "That means it's your time to die. There's no point in fighting this."

"Bring me this cursed book," Monkey roared. "Or you'll all have a taste of Monkey's iron!"

With the judges of the Courts of Death cringing before Monkey, Lord Yama had no choice but to send out the Book of the Dead. Monkey snatched it up and found his own name.

"Soul 3150," he read out loud. "This Monkey died peacefully in his sleep! Hah! That's easily solved." He grabbed a writing brush and crossed out his entry with a stroke. Then, with another stroke, he crossed out the names of all the other monkeys for good measure.

In this way, Monkey defeated death. Back in the Cave of the Waterfall, his body started breathing again. Lord Yama had no more power over him or his monkey subjects. None of them would ever die.

Delighted with his night's work, Monkey fought his way back out of the underworld, giving several thousand demons a good thrashing along the way. He woke from his dream with a happy smile. "We all will live forever!" he told his monkey subjects.

Others were less happy. The next morning,

both the Dragon King and Lord Yama sent angry letters to the Jade Emperor, the ruler of Heaven and Earth. They complained at length about the Monkey King's upstart antics.

"Who is this awful monkey?" asked the Jade Emperor, who hated being given bad news before breakfast. "How can he possibly be causing so much havoc?"

"Why don't you invite Monkey to live here, but give him a meaningless job," suggested his wife, the Queen of Heaven. "That way you can keep an eye on him, and make sure he doesn't get up to mischief."

The Jade Emperor thought it was a good plan. He summoned Monkey to Heaven. Monkey went willingly, dressed in his finest clothes. "At last I'm getting the recognition I deserve," he thought.

"I have an important job for you," the Emperor

lied. "Would you like to be my Keeper of Horses?"

Monkey readily agreed.

At first, he was delighted with his new
heavenly job. He kept the horses contented, sleek
and fat. But, after two weeks, he began to wonder
when he was going to be paid for all his hard work.

He went along to the Imperial Treasury, and

discovered that his job was not only unpaid but also very junior – so junior that it didn't even come with a proper title.

Monkey did not take this well. He ground his teeth and zipped about Heaven in a rage, breaking things. Buildings were smashed, trees were uprooted, and shards of priceless porcelain flew through the air like rain.

Various gods and immortal beings tried to stop him, but Monkey was too strong for them. He whomped them to every point on the compass, and some new ones too.

"Any more fools want to play with Monkey?" he crowed, as his pile of defeated gods grew bigger. "I'm more powerful than all of you."

By now, the Jade Emperor was becoming seriously alarmed. It seemed it would be impossible to defeat Monkey by force alone.

"If you can't beat him," whispered the Queen of Heaven, "why don't you try flattery instead?"

The Jade Emperor was desperate enough to give anything a try. He raised his voice and called out to Monkey. "O powerful Monkey King," he said. "Would you like a better job? I have just the post: how does Guardian of the Garden of the Peaches of Immortality sound? It is a very important position."

"Does it come with a title?" said Monkey. "It had better be a proper one. Or I'll bash..."

"You can call yourself 'Great Sage, Equal of Heaven' if you like," said the Emperor quickly.

"I like that," said Monkey. "Because it's true."

For a short time, there was peace in Heaven. Monkey's job was very easy. He got to laze about in the garden all day, and feast with his friends all night. He was very pleased with his new title

too. There
was only one
problem: the
Peaches of
Immortality only
ripened once every six thousand
years, and they were coming into fruit
right now. Every day, the Great Sage
watched the fruit grow fatter and juicier, and
dreamed of gobbling them up.

In the end, he couldn't help himself. He
climbed into the trees and gorged himself on
peaches till the glorious, sticky juice ran down
his chin and matted his fur.

"These taste like moonbeams and rainbows!"
he sighed, as he gobbled another and another.
Finally, with a full belly, he fell asleep amongst

the branches.

The Queen of Heaven always held a party to celebrate the ripening of the Peaches of Immortality. When her maids came to collect the fruit, they woke Monkey from his nap.

"Great Sage, where have all the peaches gone?" asked the maids.

Monkey pretended he didn't know. "Why do you want them?" he asked.

"We need them for the Queen's party," answered the maid.

"What party? Why haven't I been invited?!" Monkey roared. "This is an outrage. The Queen has made a huge mistake!"

Preparations were being made all over Heaven for the party. Monkey smashed them to smithereens. Huge tureens of jade punch – a delicious and powerful drink – had been laid out

in the banquet hall. Monkey downed the lot.
The great sage Lao Tzu had prepared cauldrons of
his special immortality pills. Monkey swallowed
them all. He pulled down the garlands and popped
all the balloons. Then he ran away from Heaven,
back home to the Cave of the Waterfall.

This time, the Emperor sent his armies to try
and capture Monkey. But, fortified by the peaches,
the jade punch and the pills, even hundreds of
thousands of soldiers and powerful generals
couldn't beat Monkey now.

Using magic, Monkey turned each of his hairs
into another armed, angry monkey. With this army
at his back, he charged into battle and began
thrashing the Emperor's troops left, right,
forwards, backwards and upside down.

"It's time to step down, you empty Emperor!"
Monkey cried, brandishing his iron pillar. "You're

second best. MONKEY is Number One!"

Fortunately Buddha, the most powerful being in the universe, had been invited to the party. He arrived to find Heaven in uproar.

"What is going on?" asked Buddha. "Where are all the other guests?"

The Jade Emperor explained that the party was cancelled. Worse still, because Monkey had drunk and eaten every kind of immortality potion going, he was practically invincible.

"Let me deal with this," said Buddha calmly. He glided down on a cloud to Flower Fruit Mountain. All the fighting stopped when he arrived. On Earth, he was so tall that his head scraped the sky.

"Monkey King, I would like to speak with you." Buddha held out his hand, and Monkey climbed on. "How about a challenge?" Buddha went on. "You can be ruler of Heaven if you can somersault off my hand. If you can't, you will have to accept your punishment for all the trouble you've caused."

"You're on!" said Monkey. "That's easy-peasy." For while Buddha's giant hand was pretty big, Monkey knew he could fly thousands of miles in the blink of an eye. He set off with a great leap, zooming through the air so fast that the whole world turned into a blur.

When he'd been tumbling for a while, he saw five great pink pillars rising up into the air.

"Ah! These must be the pillars at the end of the world," thought Monkey. "That'll do."

He landed, went up to the largest pillar and scratched "Monkey was here" with his iron rod. Then he peed on the pillar for good measure. Thoroughly satisfied at a job done well, he

zoomed back to Buddha.

"I went further than anyone's ever gone before," he boasted. "Say hello to the new Emperor of Heaven."

"What nonsense," said Buddha. "You never left my hand."

"Impossible!" Monkey looked down at Buddha's hand. He could hardly believe his eyes.

There, at the base of the middle finger, was something that looked like tiny writing. Peering closer, Monkey saw that it was his signature, scratched by his own hand only moments ago. Even worse, there was a strong whiff of monkey urine.

For the first time in his life, Monkey was at a loss for words. He tried to somersault away – but Buddha plucked him out of the air and placed a mountain over his head. It didn't hurt, because

Monkey was too tough, but there was absolutely no chance of escape. With the Jade Emperor and all his heavenly armies cheering him on, Buddha sealed the mountain tight with a spell so that it couldn't be moved.

"Stay there, Monkey," said Buddha. "And have a good, hard think about changing your ways. If you manage it, maybe one day I'll set you free."

And there, beneath the dark and lonely mountain, unable to eat or sleep or even move, Monkey sat for a very long time indeed.

In Chinese, the word for New Year is Guo Nian,
meaning "to overcome Nian". This is the legend
of Nian and how he was overcome.

The New Year Monster

Long ago, when the land was wilder and people were fewer, there lived a fearful sea monster named Nian. A mighty hunter, Nian had long horns, sharp claws and even sharper teeth. He spent most of the year sleeping in the dark, oozy mud of the ocean depths. But once a year, on New Year's Eve – which in China marks the beginning of spring – he came ashore to feed.

Then, Nian would roam through remote
coastal villages, looking for food. He would devour
any crops in the ground, any unwary animals and
even any people unlucky enough to cross his path.
Snap – gobble – gulp! They were gone.

People everywhere lived in fear of Nian. As the
awful date approached, some would hide inside
their houses, board up their doors and windows,
and pray that the monster would not find a way in.
Others fled high into the mountains, hoping to get
too far from the sea for him to follow.

In one small village, as people hammered
boards over their windows and packed up bundles
to carry into the mountains, a woman noticed a
man with long white hair, leaning on a stick and
watching her curiously.

"I don't know who you are, sir, but it is not safe
to stay here tonight," she warned him.

"Why is that?" asked the man unruffled.

"The monster Nian is coming," she replied.
"He will devour anyone he finds here. You should
flee to the mountains like me, or at least take
refuge in my house – and be sure not to open
a door or window until morning has broken."

The old man smiled. "I do not fear any
monster," he told her. "But I thank you for
your kindness."

The New Year Monster

"In return," the man went on, "I will protect your village from this Nian."

"You don't understand," moaned the woman. "You can't defeat a monster like Nian. If you stay here, he will crunch you up like a cookie! Please, please, come with me to the mountains where you will be safe."

But the man only smiled and shook his head. Nothing the woman said made any difference. Eventually, not daring to linger behind any longer, she left. "Be careful," she called, as she set off.

"Don't worry," said the man, with a cheerful wave. "I'll be fine – and so will your village. This time, your monster won't know what's waiting for him," he chuckled to himself. He glanced around the village with a keen eye, then set to work.

First, he went out to the woods and cut a huge bundle of bamboo sticks, and another one of firewood, which he carried back and stacked neatly in the village square. To these, he added a pile of heavy old metal pots, pans and cans, borrowed from the village houses.

Then he sat down and, rummaging in his cloak, pulled out a packet of scarlet paper. Deftly, he cut and folded many of the sheets into cheerful paper lanterns, which he hung among the trees. The rest, he decorated with poems and expressions of good fortune. These, he pasted over doors and in windows, until the village looked ready for a festival, not a monster.

Finally, as the sun began to sink, the man returned to the square and built a bonfire from the waiting firewood. Soon, orange-and-gold flames were darting merrily upwards, filling the darkness with warmth and light and occasional showers of sparks. The man wrapped his cloak tightly around his shoulders and settled down to wait.

In the briny depths of the ocean, Nian stirred. A rumble of hunger had disturbed his year-long sleep. Two cold, round eyes blinked open. Slowly, he shook his scaly bulk free of seaweed and slime. It was time to feed. With heavy steps, he sloshed ashore, heading for the nearest village... the village where the old man was waiting patiently.

The sky above the village was dark, but not the deep, blinding dark Nian was used to, and there were more surprises in store once he reached the village itself. Nian had been expecting to find the houses dark and shuttered, and smelling of fear. Instead, he was greeted by bright lanterns and gaily decorated houses.

Wondering uneasily what was going on, he cast about for something or someone to eat. He sniffed the air deeply and caught the scent of old man... Licking his lips, he followed the scent until it mingled with another smell – woodsmoke!

Nian sneezed as the smoke tickled his nose. Then he rounded a corner and blinked in the unaccustomed brightness. In the middle of the village square, flames leaped and crackled, dazzling his eyes, which were used to darkness and cold, watery views.

Nian roared with confusion. His roar was met by another, even louder noise...

CLATTER! BANG! CRASH!

The old man was drumming on the pots and pans, and banging lids together, making a terrible racket. Nian shook his head, trying to clear his ears. When he looked again, there was a figure

standing fearlessly right in front of him. Nian
bared his long, yellowy fangs in a snarl...

POP! CRACK! BANG!

The sound was like gunfire, although in truth
it was just bamboo sticks exploding on the fire
(which is what happens if you burn bamboo).

It was too much for Nian who, like most
monsters, was a coward at heart. He turned and
ran, back to the muddy ocean depths, while the old
man laughed and laughed.

When the villagers returned the next day, they
were amazed to find their village completely

untouched,
except for the
red paper lanterns
swinging from the tree
branches, and the red paper
poems adorning their houses.

Then the woman who had tried to warn the old man spotted him sitting peacefully in the square.

"You did it!" she exclaimed. "But I don't understand... HOW did you defeat the monster?"

The old man laughed at her shock. "It's not difficult when you know," he said modestly. And he explained they could drive Nian away every new year, with lanterns and loud noises and plenty of bright decorations.

In order to share the good news, the villagers dressed up in their best clothes and went to visit their friends and family; and so the news spread, and everyone learned how to defeat the monster.

Now, on New Year's Eve, people still hang lanterns, paste up red paper decorations and set off firecrackers (which are even noiser than burning bamboo). Houses blaze with light and people stay up to welcome the New Year and celebrate together, without fear of Nian and his terrible hunger.

Usborne Quicklinks

For links to websites where you can find out more about China's traditional folk tales, festivals and the art of brush and ink painting, go to the Usborne Quicklinks website at **www.usborne.com/quicklinks** and enter the keywords "Stories from China". Please follow the online safety guidelines at the Usborne Quicklinks website.

Designed by Lenka Hrehova & Tabitha Blore
Digital manipulation: Nick Wakeford
Edited by Rosie Dickins & Lesley Sims

Illustrations arranged and contents developed in association with Jieli Publishing House Co., Ltd., China.